CARMINA, COME DANCE!

CARMINA, COME DANCE!

by Mary K. Whittington
illustrated by Michael McDermott

ATHENEUM   1989   NEW YORK

For Jane Yolen, with love and thanks
M. K. W.

Atheneum
Macmillan Publishing Company
866 Third Avenue, New York, NY 10022
Collier Macmillan Canada, Inc.
First Edition
Printed in Hong Kong by South China Printing Co.
10   9   8   7   6   5   4   3   2   1

Library of Congress Cataloging-in-Publication Data

Whittington, Mary K.
Carmina, come dance! / Mary K. Whittington. — 1st ed.
p.   cm.
Summary: Carmina is afraid of her great-grandmother until the old
lady plays the piano and Carmina discovers that the music makes a
special bond between them.
ISBN 0-689-31554-6
[1. Great-grandmothers—Fiction.   2. Music—Fiction.   3. Old age—
Fiction.]   I. Title.
PZ7.W6188Car   1989
[E]—dc19
88-34430   CIP   AC

Carmina's great-grandmother has come. Beneath her yellow shawl, her dress is gray as dust. She is old, old, the oldest lady Carmina has ever seen.

Afraid, she hides beneath the piano, but Great-Grandmother sits down and begins to play. Carmina shuts her eyes, pretends she is alone…

in her secret cave among the roots of three great trees. Birds trill in
the forest. Carmina hears a rumbling, growing, growing until
the earth trembles and the trees shake with thunder.

Up gallops a chestnut stallion. His trappings ring golden with bells.

Carmina leaps to the saddle, grabs handfuls of mane. The stallion runs through forest and meadow, splashes through pools, and races the river. Ever the bells, ringing their song, sing with the thunder of galloping hooves.

The stallion runs down a valley between icy
mountains, toward the red-tiled roofs of a harbor town.

Carmina holds tight to his mane. He clatters down
cobblestone streets. At the wharf a ship awaits.

Into a silver sunset they sail. The wind sings them
to sleep beneath strange stars.

At dawn, the ship moors at a cloud-cloaked island.
Carmina and the stallion canter up to a great
stone house.

Dismounting, Carmina tiptoes into a high hall. All is
gray—pillars, walls, tapestries, the flagstone floor.

A lady sleeps on a chair by a window. Her hair lies like a shawl around her shoulders. Her gown is gray.

She awakens. She is young, young. "Welcome, Carmina," she says.
"Do you know me?" asks Carmina.

The lady smiles, and the harp in the corner begins to
play rippling waltzes.

"Come dance, Carmina. One-two-three, one-two-three."

Hand in hand, Carmina and the lady twirl until they
are dizzy with laughter.

"Look," says the lady, "you bring color to my gray house. Stay with me always, pretty Carmina."

"No," says Carmina, "I have to go home. Why don't you come ride with me to my cave in the forest?"

The lady looks sad and points out the window, where dark clouds churn the sky. "The Storm will never let me go"

"The Storm will never catch us," Carmina shouts.
She pulls the lady outside. They leap to the stallion's
back. Away they gallop down to the ship.

The Storm howls and blasts them seaward. It shreds the sails with shrieking gusts, pursues with waterspouts. It hides the harbor of the town with curtains made of rain.

But the wind sets the tower bells clanging,
guiding the ship to its haven.

Carmina and the lady spring to the stallion's back.
He dashes through the town and up the valley. The
Storm hurls blinding swarms of snowflakes, raises
drifts to block the way.

But the saddle's bells ring warm as sunshine and
melt the snow.

Into the forest the stallion races. The Storm grows
dark and lashes with lightning. The forest flames.

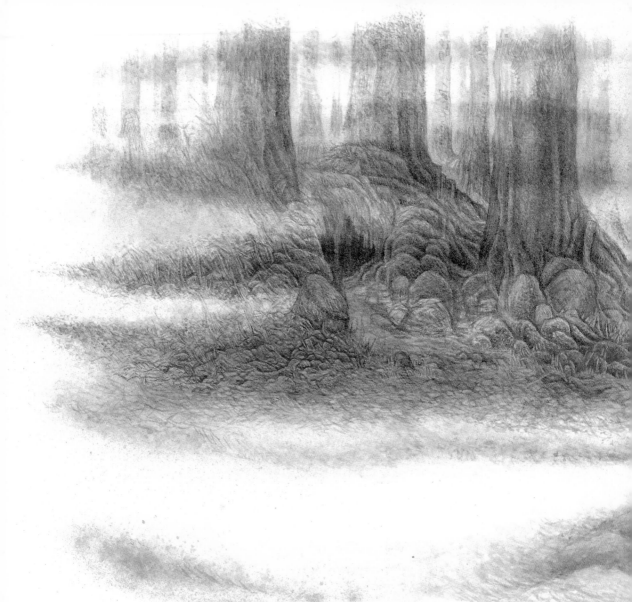

But the lady sings, her voice like bells. The Storm
weeps, quenching the fire, then blows away.

The stallion reaches the secret cave. Carmina and
the lady dismount and go inside. They watch the
stallion gallop away, the rumbling of his hooves fading,
fading until Carmina can no longer hear him. A bird
trills in the branches above.